FROM THE LIBRARY OF

Tanya Ladowicz

YOU CAN BE A DETECTIVE, TOO

Scratch and **sniff** each clue,
and follow the scent with Detective Arthur.

Detective Arthur on the Scent

by Mary J. Fulton
pictures by Aurelius Battaglia

*from Daddy
to Tanya
7 years old*

GOLDEN PRESS • NEW YORK

Western Publishing Company, Inc.

On Arthur's birthday, a very special package came from his grandmother. It was a detective kit, with a detective hat, a magnifying glass, and a detecting book. Arthur was delighted.

His mother made a chocolate birthday cake with chocolate icing, and after Arthur licked the bowl, he put on his detective hat and went out to buy some birthday candles.

When he came back, the cake was gone!
"My birthday cake has been stolen!" howled
Arthur, and he ran to tell his mother.
"Well, Arthur," she said, "why don't you use
your brand-new detective kit to find the robbers?"

Arthur looked in his detective book to see what to do. This is what he read: "Rule 1—Search the scene of the crime for any strange objects. These may be clues. Rule 2—If a clue is a clue you can smell, you should take a big whiff of it and follow the scent."

Arthur did find a clue. It was a fat banana, right in the middle of the cake plate.

"My first clue," said Arthur, and he took a big whiff of the banana and followed the scent out the back door.

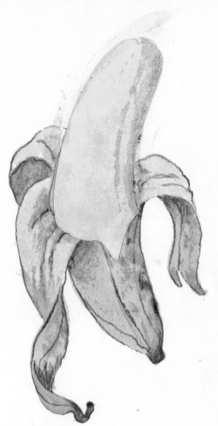

Scratch and sniff
the banana Arthur found.
Turn the page to see
where the scent will lead him.

The scent led over the picket fence into Darwin's yard, and there was Darwin, sitting in a rocker, holding a bunch of bananas very like the banana clue. But there was no chocolate birthday cake to be seen.

Arthur looked in his book. "Rule 3," he read. "If you see a suspicious-looking character, question him slyly."

"Okay, Darwin," said Arthur, "hand over my birthday cake!"

"What birthday cake?" asked Darwin.

Arthur looked in his book again. "Rule 4," he read. "If the suspect refuses to talk, look for another clue and take him along for questioning."

Arthur found a cherry lollipop on the windowsill. "Hmmm," he said, "why would this lollipop be on the windowsill unless it is a clue? Darwin, you'll have to come along for questioning. Please follow me."

Arthur took a big sniff of the clue, and followed the cherry scent.

Scratch and sniff the cherry lollipop. Where will the scent of this clue lead?

The scent led out the gate and down Main Street to the park. There was Millicent, sitting on a park bench, with a bag full of cherry lollipops. But there was no birthday cake to be seen.

"First I question the suspect," Arthur whispered to himself. "Now, Millicent," he said sternly, "what have you done with my birthday cake?"

"What birthday cake?" asked Millicent.

"She won't talk," said Arthur to himself, "so now I look around for another clue."

He found a very suspicious lemon under the bench. "Oho," said Arthur, "anything that is suspicious is likely to be a clue. Please follow me, Millicent, I'm taking you along for questioning."

Arthur took a sniff of the lemon, and trotted off, following the scent.

Scratch and sniff
the lemon that Arthur found.
Will this clue lead him to
the missing birthday cake?

The scent led across the street and around the corner to the school playground. And there was Samson, sitting at the bottom of the slide, holding a pitcher of lemonade.

"Aha!" barked Arthur. "Lemon—lemonade! The trail is getting hot. Samson, give me my birthday cake."

"What birthday cake?" asked Samson.

"Oh dear," said Arthur, "you won't confess either. You'll have to come along for questioning, too. But first, I must search for another clue."

There was a grape jelly sandwich on the seesaw. "This must be a clue," said Arthur.

He sniffed the grape jelly and ran into the woods behind the school.

Scratch and sniff the grape jelly. Turn the page to see if Arthur will find his birthday cake.

The scent led along a trail, and over a stream. "Hurry up," Arthur called to the suspects, "there's no time to waste." They pushed through some bushes, and there, sitting in a tree, was Amelia, with a basket of grape jelly sandwiches.

"Amelia," said Arthur, "I demand my birthday cake!"

"What birthday cake?" asked Amelia, and she took a mint ice cream cone from behind her back and licked it.

Scratch and sniff
the mint ice cream,
and turn the page to see
who stole the birthday cake.

"I'm getting very discouraged," said Arthur, "but I won't give up yet!"

He looked about for another clue. "Wait a minute!" he cried. "Ice cream in the woods? That's a clue! You're coming in for questioning, Amelia. Follow me."

Off he galloped, following the mint scent, with the suspects rushing along behind.

They crashed through a thicket, and stopped short at the edge of a sparkling pond. There, by the pond, sitting on a table with a big barrel of mint ice cream, was Wallace.

"Please, Wallace," said Arthur with a sigh, "where is my delicious birthday cake with the chocolate icing?"

"What birthday cake?" asked Wallace, and he grinned.

"Well," growled Arthur, gritting his teeth, "if my cake isn't here, there must be another clue."

But look and sniff as he would, Arthur could not find another clue.

"Oh," he cried, "no clues, no cake," and he threw his detective hat into the bushes. "I'm a terrible detective, and what's worse, I'm a detective without a birthday cake."

"Surprise, surprise!" cried all the suspects, and several more of Arthur's friends who came popping out from behind some trees. "Happy Birthday!"

And there was the birthday cake. There was writing on it now. "Happy Birthday, Detective Arthur," it read. "Oh, my," said Arthur, and he sniffed his birthday cake. "Mmmm, I do love chocolate!"

Scratch and sniff
this piece of Arthur's cake.
Do you like chocolate, too?

Happy Birthday
Detective Arthur

The suspects put all the food they had been carrying on the table.

Then everyone ate and ate, until they were all so filled with bananas, and lemonade, and cherry lollipops, and grape jelly sandwiches, and mint ice cream, and chocolate cake, that all they could do was lean back and sigh.

"Oh, my," said Arthur, with his detective hat back on, "this is the nicest party a detective ever had. And these are the yummiest clues a detective ever ate!"

A B C D